For Piers and Tom.
J. N.

First United States edition 1992

Margaret K. McElderry Books
Macmillan Publishing Company
866 Third Avenue
New York, NY 10022

Macmillan Publishing Company is part of the Maxwell Communication Group of Companies.

Text copyright © 1991 by Margaret Mahy
Illustrations copyright © 1991 by Jan Nesbitt
First published by J. M. Dent & Sons Ltd., London
Printed in Italy
10 9 8 7 6 5 4 3 2 1
Library of Congress Catalog Card Number: 91-62222
ISBN 0-689-50547-7

"The Witch Dog," "Teddy and the Witches," and "The Boy Who Went Looking for a Friend" first published in *The First Margaret Mahy Story Book*, copyright © Margaret Mahy, 1972. "Kite Saturday," "Mrs Bartelmy's Pet," "Telephone Detectives" and "Patrick Comes to School" first published in *The Second Margaret Mahy Story Book*, copyright © Margaret Mahy, 1973. "A Tall Story," "Aunt Nasty," "The Breakfast Bird" and "Looking for a Ghost" first published in *The Third Margaret Mahy Story Book*, copyright © Margaret Mahy, 1975.

MARGARET MAHY

A TALL STORY

and other tales

illustrated by JAN NESBITT

Margaret K. McElderry Books
New York

Maxwell Macmillan International
New York   Oxford   Singapore   Sydney

Contents

A Tall Story

Susan was the family storyteller, and Richard was the family listener. She told the stories and he always listened.

But when Uncle Ted came to call, it turned out he was a storyteller too, and Richard stopped listening to Susan. He listened to Uncle Ted all the time — one story after another.

"Tell a story, Uncle Ted!" demanded Richard.

"Don't start him off again," begged Susan. "I think it's bad to encourage him."

"Just one little story," Richard begged.

Uncle Ted leaned back, looking up at the ceiling, as storytellers do.

"I think I've told most of my stories," he said. "Let me see! I've told you about the mystery treasure of Bones Island, haven't I?"

"That was a good one," Richard answered, smiling and re-membering.

"Oh yes . . . and I've told you about the time I was nearly married to the Queen of the Bird People?"

"She lived in a big royal nest, didn't she?" Richard said. "And laid eggs."

"What about the catching of the Great Christmas Tree Thieves?" Uncle Ted asked, thinking hard. "A smart bit of detective work on my part. All the thieves were dressed as Santa Claus."

"Hasn't anything happened to you since then?" Richard asked.

"Nothing, nothing," said Uncle Ted sadly. "Except, of course, for the hunting of the giant land-dwelling oyster. You'll remember the headlines in the paper, no doubt. You may even have seen it on TV."

"You don't hunt oysters," Susan said snappily. "You fish for them. You know you fish for them, Uncle Ted."

"Those are the small ones," Uncle Ted replied carelessly. "This was a large one. . . . Enormous! A horrible amorphous creature as big as a town hall . . . a land-dwelling oyster."

"It couldn't be," Susan said sternly. "No oyster could be as big as a town hall."

"Tell me!" begged Richard. "Tell me the story."

So Uncle Ted began: "This dreadful monster had taken to coming out at night, and snatching up all kinds of midnight travelers. Five vans of buns and assorted sweets on their way to a southern carnival had vanished off the face of the earth. Two brass bands, a traveling circus, a mobile library, and an army truck filled with angry sergeant-majors had entirely disappeared. . . . We couldn't let it continue. A creature with a digestion like that had to be gotten rid of. No one was safe—not even town councilors. Of course, they sent for me, offering to pay richly if I disposed of the monster."

Uncle Ted paused.

"You always make adventures pay," said Richard. "Go on."

"None of it is true," Susan muttered.

"I chose three guns . . . my trusty revolver, my trusty three-ought-three rifle, and my trusty 1812 cannon. I drove toward the giant oyster's lair in my little truck with the hotted-up engine. Many oyster-soup officials were standing by, with a Pre-Fabricated Re-Locatable Oyster-Soup Factory. As soon as I had shot the giant oyster they would move in with a hundred oyster-soup cooks, great vats of salt and pepper, and bags of lemons. They hoped to make a year's supply of oyster soup from this dreadful monster."

"I'll bet you planned all that," said Richard. "Were you getting money for it?"

"I was to get ten cents for every can of oyster soup. They expected to sell at least twenty cans of soup a day over a year. It was a small fortune," said Uncle Ted.

"Uncle Ted, nobody believes you," said Susan, shaking her head.

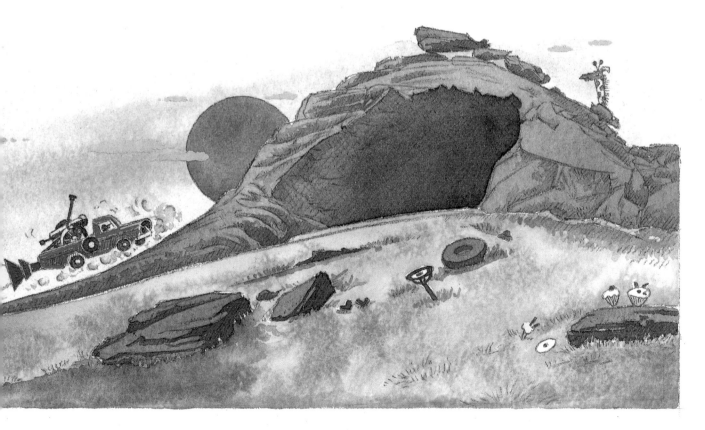

Uncle Ted went on: "I moved in first with a loudspeaker. From a distance of a mere two hundred yards I began making sarcastic remarks about oysters. This was to infuriate the oyster and bring it out into the daylight. Out it came . . . a great amorphous mass as big as a town hall."

"You've already said that," objected Susan.

"Was it horrible?" asked Richard.

"Unspeakably horrible!" Uncle Ted cried, shuddering. "It reared up menacingly over the trees, all slimy and jellylike, with great teeth gnashing in a wide slit of a mouth."

"Oysters don't have teeth," Susan stated.

"They don't usually," agreed Uncle Ted. "I can't explain it. I'm not an oyster expert. All I know is, this oyster came undulating toward me at surprising speed, gnashing a mouthful of very sharp-looking teeth. Perhaps it had made itself some false teeth out of oyster shell."

"I don't know how you can bear to listen to such things," Susan muttered to Richard, shaking her head again.

"I fired first with my trusty three-ought-three rifle, and then with my trusty revolver. I could not miss such a huge target, but mere bullets made no difference. Even when I fired the cannonball right through it, it did not hesitate. I had to climb into my truck and drive off as quickly as I could."

"But the oyster could catch trucks!" cried Susan triumphantly. "You said it had caught an army truck."

"Too true!" agreed Uncle Ted. "It nearly caught up with me, but my truck, though small, was fitted with an experimental jet engine of a revolutionary kind. Just as the oyster (a vast amorphous mass, did I mention?) was about to swoop on me, I pressed button A, and rotating helicopter blades unfolded out of the roof of my truck, whisking me out of danger. Furious at losing its prey, the terrible mollusc set up a wailing so horrible that — I give you my word — the helicopter blades nearly stopped, and I hung quivering in the air. There were a few tense moments, believe me, before I was out of reach and the oyster finally gave up and slunk back to its cave.

"There was great despondency when I returned at last to report to the council.

"'We'll have to declare a national emergency and call out the army,' declared the town councilors. The oyster-soup officials weren't too happy about this. The army could deal with it, of course, but this meant blowing the monster to bits — thus spoiling it for soup purposes. The oyster-soup officials didn't fancy picking bits of oyster out of the trees for miles around.

"We all thought hard. A quick, cool brain is worth a million in an emergency.

"'I've got a plan,' I said. 'It'll cost a bit to get it under way, and if it works I'll want fifteen cents on every can of oyster soup.'

"'You drive a hard bargain,' said the leading oyster-soup official. 'But we have no choice. If we capture this great oyster, I think we'll manage to get command of the entire oyster-soup market.'

"Now," cried Uncle Ted, "what do you think my plan was?"

"I couldn't ever guess," said Susan sourly. "It could be anything."

"Go on, Uncle Ted," whispered Richard, staring at Uncle Ted anxiously.

"All afternoon we spent loading a county sanitation truck. The hotel gave us five kegs of beer — rather a poor brew, I'm afraid. Miss

Dobbs, the vicar's sister, hearing the announcement of our plan over the radio, contributed a whole dozen bottles of her famous parsnip-and-elderberry wine. Several farmers gave large quantities of apple cider. Colonel Scobie donated several flagons of a drink of his own invention — carrot whisky, he called it. He said it helped him see in the dark, being extra rich in vitamin A. A Japanese family gave us a cask of saki — I think that's made from rice. My gift was simple, but incredibly rich — simply five cases of simple French champagne that I happened to have with me."

"Uncle Ted, your stories are all lies and boasting," cried Susan. "Lies! Lies!"

"Susan," said her mother, "you are not to call your uncle a liar. Go outside if you can't behave better."

Susan went outside. "Uncle or not, it's still all lies," she told the cat. Then she hid in the garden under the open window to listen to the rest of the story.

Inside the house, Uncle Ted went on: "Who was to drive this truck? Every eye looked hopefully at me. It was putting my head into the jaws of death yet again, but I agreed with a tired smile. We traveling adventurers are prepared for anything. Besides, I had a small fortune at stake.

"Late that night I drove the truck down the road that passed by the oyster's lair. As we had expected, the oyster charged at the truck. I saw its dark shape against the stars — a vast amorphous mass (as I just may have mentioned before) and I had time to slide out and hide in a ditch while the oyster, not realizing I had gone, swept by me and devoured the truck . . . beer, carrot whisky, cider, parsnip wine, saki, champagne, and all.

"We waited anxiously. After about a quarter of an hour the oyster began to behave in a very strange fashion. It began to sway to and fro and actually tried to sing. I can tell you, it was one of the worst half hours of my career. I've sat through operas and many folksong recitals, but nothing, nothing to compare with the giant oyster, full of champagne and carrot whisky, trying to sing. It was drunk, of course."

"An oyster drunk!" cried Richard, almost not believing.

"Hopelessly inebriated!" Uncle Ted said solemnly. "At the end of half an hour it collapsed in a quivering heap. The Pre-Fabricated Re-Locatable Oyster-Soup Factory came in, the cooks got to work and — well — you're having some of it for dinner tonight, so your mother tells me."

"Was it fair to cut it up while it was helpless?" asked Richard doubtfully.

"Not quite fair — but you can't consider fair play too strongly when you're dealing with a creature that will tackle a truck full of sergeant-majors, you know. Besides, it must have died happy — don't forget it had just consumed a year's supply of French champagne. People tasting the soup, incidentally, comment on the delicate champagne flavor that complements the oyster so beautifully. Go out into the kitchen, and get your mother to show you the genuine can."

Richard ran off, and Uncle Ted could hear him shouting excitedly in the kitchen.

"Uncle Ted," said a voice, and there was Susan. "Uncle Ted, shall I tell you how the story really ended?"

Uncle Ted looked at her cautiously. "I'd like to hear," he said.

Susan began: "There you were, driving down the road at midnight. You saw the oyster descending on the truck . . . a vast amorphous mass—"

"I like the words you choose," interrupted Uncle Ted.

"Now, now was the time for you to leap out of the truck. You started to open the door. Horrors! it was locked. It was a special automatic locking door, easy to open if you knew how to, but you had forgotten to learn how. The giant oyster was coming nearer and nearer and then — and then . . ."

"Yes! Yes!" whispered Uncle Ted.

"Alas, the monster leaped on to the truck and ate you all up. You struggled wildly, but it was no use. Later you were turned into soup, and Mother is cooking you in the kitchen right now."

"But I seem to be still here," objected Uncle Ted. "I'm sure I'm here . . ."

"All ghosts feel that," Susan said firmly. "I'm afraid, Uncle Ted, you are a mere ghostly apparition."

Uncle Ted and Susan looked at each other. . . . They began to smile. They began to laugh.

"A much better end," said Uncle Ted. "I didn't realize there was another tall-storyteller in the family."

"It's not really a better end, just a bit taller," said Susan. "Yours can be the right one. You laugh too hard for a ghost! Now, you tell your end to the story specially for me."

"I think it's time you told me a story," said Uncle Ted. "For instance, I've heard all sorts of rumors about the time you were carried off by the rare Subterranean Gorilla who had seen you swimming at the beach and had been much struck by your remarkable beauty. Wouldn't you like to tell me the facts of the case? You might have time before the soup is served."

So Susan told him that story and, as it turned out, Uncle Ted was a wonderful listener — all good storytellers have to be — even better than Richard.

Aunt Nasty

"Oh dear!" said Mother, one lunch time, after she had finished reading a letter the postman had just left.

"What's the matter?" asked Father. Even Toby and Claire looked up from their boiled eggs.

"Aunt Nasty has written to say she is coming to stay with us," said Mother. "The thought of it makes me worried."

"You must tell her we will be out!" cried Toby. He did not like the sound of Aunt Nasty.

"Or say we have no room," said Father.

"You know I can't do that," said Mother. "Remember, Aunt Nasty is a *witch*."

Toby and Claire looked at each other with round eyes. They had forgotten, for a moment, that Aunt Nasty was a witch as well as being an aunt. If they said there was no room in the house Aunt Nasty might be very cross. She might turn them into frogs.

"She is arriving on the plane tomorrow," said Mother, looking at the letter. "It is hard to read this witch-writing. She writes it with a magpie's feather, and all the letters look like broomsticks."

"I see she has written it on mouse skin," said Father.

"Isn't she just showing off?" asked Toby. "If she was a real witch she would ride a broomstick here . . . not come in a plane."

Claire had to move into Toby's room so that Aunt Nasty would have a bedroom all to herself. She put a vase of flowers in the room, but they were not garden flowers. Aunt Nasty liked flowers of a poisonous kind, like woody nightshade and foxgloves.

"Leave the cobwebs in that corner," said Father. "Remember how cross she was when you swept them down last time. She loves dust and cobwebs. All witches do."

The next afternoon they went to the airport to meet Aunt Nasty. It was easy to see her in the crowd getting off the plane. She was one of the old sort of witches, all in black, with a pointed hat and a broomstick.

"Hello, Aunt Nasty," said Mother. "How nice to see you again."

"I don't suppose you really are pleased to see me," said Aunt Nasty, "but that doesn't matter. There is a special meeting of witches in the city this week. That is why I had to come. I will be out every night on my broom, and trying to sleep during the day. I hope the children are quiet."

"Why didn't you come on your broom, Aunt Nasty?" asked Toby. "Why did you have to come in the airplane?"

"Don't you ever listen to the weather report on the radio?" replied Aunt Nasty crossly. "It said there would be fresh winds in the Cook Strait area, increasing to gale force at midday. It isn't much fun riding a broomstick in a fresh wind, let me tell you. Even the silly airplane bucked around. I began to think they'd put us into a wheelbarrow by mistake. Two people were sick."

"Poor people," said Claire.

"Serves them right!" Aunt Nasty muttered. "People with weak stomachs annoy me."

When they got home Aunt Nasty went straight to her room. She smiled at the sight of the foxgloves and the woody nightshade, but she did not say thank you.

"I will have a catnap," she said, stroking the raggy black fur collar she wore. "I hope the bed is not damp or lumpy. I used to enjoy a damp bed when I was a young witch, but I'm getting old now."

Then she shut the door. They heard her put her suitcase against it.

"What a rude aunt!" said Toby.

"She has to be rude, because of being a witch," said Mother. "Now, do be nice quiet children, won't you! Don't make her cross, or she might turn you into tadpoles."

The children went out to play, but they were not happy.

"I don't like Aunt Nasty," said Claire.

"I don't like having a witch in the house," said Toby.

The house was very, very quiet and strange while Aunt Nasty was there. Everyone spoke in whispery voices and went around on tiptoe. Aunt Nasty stayed in her room most of the time. Once, she came out of her room and asked for some toadstools. Toby found some for her under a pine tree at the top of the hill — fine red ones with spots, but Aunt Nasty was not pleased with them.

"These are dreadful toadstools," she said. "They look good but they are quite disappointing. The brown, slimy ones are much better. You can't trust a boy to do anything properly these days. But I suppose I will have to make do with them."

That was on Tuesday. Some smoke came out of the keyhole on Wednesday, and on Thursday Aunt Nasty broke a soup plate. However, they did not see her again until Friday. Then she came out and complained that there was not enough pepper in the soup.

At last it was Sunday. Aunt Nasty had been there a week. Now she was going home again — this time by broomstick. Toby and Claire were very pleased. Mother was pleased too, and yet she looked tired and sad. She went out to take some plants to the woman next door. While she was out Father came in from the garden.

"Do you know what?" he said to Toby and Claire. "I have just remembered something. It is your mother's birthday today and we have forgotten all about it. That is what comes of having a witch in the house. We must go and buy her birthday presents at once."

"But it's Sunday, Daddy!" cried Claire. "All the shops will be shut!"

"What on earth shall we do?" asked Father. "There must be some way of getting a present for her."

"A present!" said a voice. "Who wants a present?" It was Aunt Nasty with her suitcase, a broomstick, and a big black cat at her heels.

"Oh, look at the cat!" cried Claire. "I did not know you had a cat, Aunt Nasty."

"He sits around my neck when we ride in the bus or the plane," said Aunt Nasty proudly. "It is his own idea, and it is a good one, because people think he is a fur collar and I do not have to buy a ticket for him. But what is this I hear? Have you really forgotten to buy your mother a birthday present?"

"I'm afraid we have!" said Father sadly.

"Ha!" said Aunt Nasty fiercely. "Now, I never ever forgot my mother's birthday. I always had some little gift for her. Once I gave her the biggest, blackest rat you ever saw. It was a fine rat and I would have liked it for my own pet, but nothing was too good for my mother. I let her have it."

"I don't think Mommy would like a rat," said Claire.

"I wasn't going to give her one!" snapped Aunt Nasty. "Tell me, can you children draw?"

"Yes," said Toby and Claire.

"Can you draw a birthday cake, Jell-O, little cakes, sandwiches, roast chickens, bottles of fizzy lemonade, balloons, favors, pretty flowers, birds and butterflies . . . and presents, too?"

"Yes!" said Toby and Claire.

"Well then, you draw them," said Aunt Nasty, "and I will cook up some magic. Where is the stove? Hmmm! I see it is an electric stove. It is a bit on the clean side, isn't it? An old black stove is of much more use to a witch. Mind you, I've no use for the witch who can't make do with what she can get. I will work something out, you see if I don't."

Claire drew and Toby drew. They covered lots and lots of pages with drawings of cakes and balloons and presents wrapped in pretty paper.

Aunt Nasty came in with a smoking saucepan. "Give me your drawings," she said. "Hurry up, I haven't got all day. Hmmm! They aren't very good, are they? But they'll have to do. A good witch can manage with a scribble if she has to."

She popped the drawings into the saucepan where they immediately caught fire and burned to ashes. A thick blue smoke filled the room. No one could see anyone else.

"This smoke tastes like birthday cake," called Claire.

"It tastes like Jell-O and ice cream," said Toby. The smoke began to go away up the chimney.

"I smell flowers," said Father.

Then they saw that the whole room was changed.

Everywhere there were leaves and flowers, and birds only as big as your little fingernail. The table was covered with Jell-O of all

colors, and little cakes, and sandwiches. There was a trifle pudding and two roasted chickens. There were huge wooden dishes of fruit — even grapes, cherries, and pineapples. There was a big silver bowl of fizzy lemonade with rose petals floating in it. All around the table were presents and favors and balloons — so many of them that they came up to the children's knees.

"Aha!" said Aunt Nasty, looking pleased. "I haven't lost my touch with a bit of pretty magic."

Best of all was the birthday cake. It was so big there was no room for it on the table. It stood like a pink-and-white mountain by the fireplace. The balloons bounced and floated around the room. The tiny birds flew everywhere, singing. One of them made a nest as small as a thimble in a vase of flowers.

"What is in this package?" asked Claire, pointing to a package that moved and rustled. "Is it a rat?"

"It's two pigeons," said Aunt Nasty. "There is a pigeon house for them in one of the other packages. Well, I must be off. I've wasted enough time. The saucepan is spoiled by the way, but you won't mind that. It was a nasty cheap one, anyhow."

"Won't you stay and wish Mommy a happy birthday?" asked

Toby. "She would like to say thank you for her birthday party."

"Certainly not!" said Aunt Nasty. "I never ever say thank you myself. I don't expect anyone to say it to me. I love rudeness, but that is because I am a witch. You are not witches, so make sure you are polite to everybody." She tied her suitcase to her broomstick with string, and her cat climbed on to her shoulder.

"Good-bye to you, anyway," she said. "I don't like children, but you are better than most. Perhaps I will see you again, or perhaps I won't." She climbed onto her broomstick and flew out of the window, her suitcase bobbing behind her. She was a bit wobbly.

"Well," said Father, "she wasn't so bad after all. It will be strange not having a witch in the house anymore."

"Mother will love her birthday," said Claire. "It was good of Aunt Nasty. It is the prettiest party I have ever seen."

"I don't even mind if she visits us again next year," said Toby.

"Look, there is Mommy coming now," said Father. "Let's go and meet her."

They all ran out into the sunshine shouting, "Happy Birthday!" Toby had a quick look up in the air for Aunt Nasty. There, far above him, he saw a tiny little black speck that might have been Aunt Nasty, or it might have been a sea gull. He was not quite sure. Then he took one of Mother's hands, and Claire took the other, and they pulled her, laughing and happy, up the steps into her birthday room.

Kite Saturday

Today was Kite Saturday. Today was the day when the children took their kites up into the hills and set them flying — strange, bright birds in a pale sky. John ran and Dick ran. Sally, Lily, and Marigold ran. From under their arms streamed raggle-taggle kite tails, bowing and dancing to a secret music. Every child had a kite and every kite had a child. Together they bobbed and ran to the hills, which were free and windy and wide enough to hold them all.

Behind all the other children ran Joan. Her fingers were too clumsy to make a kite, to cut and glue the paper and stretch the string. She did not have a father or brother to do this for her. However, hard and round in the palm of her hand she had a silver coin which her mother had given her.

"Get yourself a little treat," she had said, for she knew Joan was disappointed at having no kite to fly. With the silver coin, Joan could buy an ice-cream cone or a glass of orange juice. With the silver coin, she could buy a pink sugar mouse, with a tail of green angelica. A piece of silver has its own silver magic. Still, on Kite Saturday a kite is the most magical thing of all.

On a street corner in town sat an old woman beside a straw basket, watching the children stream past to the hills. No child but Joan saw her because the autumn wind ran in front of them wearing a patchwork cloak made of red and yellow leaves, and they were following the wind. No child but Joan read the notice on her straw basket — *Lucky-Dip. Wishes and Dreams.*

Joan stopped. "Is it *really* full of wishes and dreams?" she asked the old woman.

"You have to pay a silver coin to find out, you see," the old woman said. She smoked a pipe, this old woman — and her eyes were as still and gray as stones. She puffed out blue smoke, and watched Joan through it.

"*Everyone* would want to dip," said Joan.

"Ah, yes, but I go only to the lonely places," said the old woman, "or places where people are hurrying past me."

"You can't get many silver coins that way," said Joan.

"No, but the ones I am given are special ones," the old woman told her.

Joan held out her silver coin and the old woman took it. She looked at it, bit it, and smiled a little.

"You may have a dip!" she said.

The lucky-dip smelled of hay and sawdust. Joan wriggled her fingers down into it, feeling for a package. She felt first one and then another. She was just going to take the second one, when a third package pushed its way into her hand. It was as if that package were telling her, "Take *me*! I'm the *special* one." So Joan took it. It was quite small and wrapped in silver paper.

"Don't open it until you get to the hills," the old woman said. "That's a package that needs space."

"It's only a little one," Joan remarked.

"Still, it needs space," the old woman replied sternly. "A herd of elephants might live contentedly in a walnut shell, while a particular mouse might need all the space between the stars."

Joan did not understand what the old woman was saying.

23

"I'm going to watch the kites fly," she said. "I'll open it in the hills."

But the old woman merely put her pipe back in her mouth and rested her elbows on her knees and her chin in her hands. Her eyes stared out of her brown face, much like stones that are half buried in the earth stare at the stars.

Up in the hills the children were getting ready to fly their kites. The wind came down the slope to meet them, head over heels, tumbling like an acrobat and laughing like a clown. It lifted the first kites high into the air and higher still. All the time it piped among the rocks, full of conceit at its own cleverness.

Sitting on a smooth stone, warm in the sun, Joan opened her silver package. As she turned back the last folds, something struggled and moved, something opened up under her hands.

It was a kite Joan was holding — a kite which had unfolded from her lucky-dip package! It was taller than Joan herself, and had for a tail a chain of leaves and berries and flowers. Painted on its green silk was a wild laughing face, such as the wind itself might wear.

The other children were flying their kites now. Their lines stretched through the air like the strings of a great fiddle — one only the wind could play. The wind was delighted to see Joan's big kite and came eagerly to meet her.

"Look at Joan's kite!" a child called. "It's the biggest of all."

"Look at Joan's kite!" the other children shouted. "It's going higher and higher."

The wind lifted the kite.

It lifted Joan too.

Joan was not afraid. She felt quite safe. The smell of autumn, of falling leaves and sun-warmed grass, rose around her as she soared up the clear hill of the air, dangling on the silver string of her kite. Then the wind brought her, like a little extra present, the sharp salt smell of the sea.

The hill opened up beneath her like green flowers, and suddenly she could see over them. She could see to the very edge of the world. Between Joan and the hills and the edge of the world was a blue

24

field where lines of white unicorns charged and danced. No — it wasn't a blue field . . . it was the sea, and the white unicorns were tossing waves.

"Wishes and dreams!" said the wind. "Wishes and dreams."

It was Kite Saturday and a beautiful day.

But even Kite Saturday must end. Even the wind grows tired. Falling with the autumn leaves, down came the kites out of the sky. Down came Joan on the end of her silvery string. She felt the grass under her feet. Fluttering and bowing, her kite slid down behind her, dancing while it could, watching her with eyes as golden as an owl's.

The other children crowded around her.

"What did it feel like, flying?" they asked her, but Joan could not tell them exactly.

"A bit like floating — a bit like swinging, just before you swing down again. From up in the air the hills were like green flowers, and over the hills I could see the sea."

Suddenly the wind leaped up and away from them, shouting and clapping its hands and turning cartwheels from one hilltop to another. He had forgotten the children and their kites. He was playing his own secret games again. Tired and happy, the children sighed and smiled and turned home, the kite tails hanging quietly over their arms.

Kite Saturday was over.

25

Telephone Detectives

As he dug among the tough, spreading roots in the bamboo corner, Monty heard something clink against the spade. A moment later he turned up a little black metal box — treasure! — something he had often dreamed of finding. He knew it was treasure, and it crossed his mind that it was funny that he should find treasure this day of all days.

Today was the day of the school picnic. The children of Deepford, in New Zealand, were going over the hills to the beach, for swimming, sandwiches, cakes, lemonade — and a treasure hunt. All the children had gone, except Monty. Monty had watched the buses and cars go by full of children, and then he had gone around to the back fence because he just could not bear it any longer. He had sat down among the bamboos in the bamboo corner and felt sad, in a hot and angry kind of way.

Monty had chicken pox. There were a few spots on his face, but mostly they were under his shirt, all itching away like mad. Monty wished he felt really sick, then he wouldn't want to go on a picnic. As it was, apart from the itches, he felt quite well and full of longings — especially for the treasure hunt. Nothing seemed fair. In a horrid way he enjoyed feeling miserable and being angry at the other children who didn't have chicken pox. He lay on the warm ground under the bamboos and sulked.

But that was some time ago, for Monty's thoughts had slowly changed. First, he had started thinking that the day was beautiful. Then he had noticed a bird hopping on the lawn. A spider swung on its thread, and a tiny little atom of a grub looped itself madly up a

thick bamboo stem. All those things are busy, thought Monty, and none of them knows or cares that I'm here, feeling sad . . .

Yet the sight of these tiny restless creatures, all doing something, had made Monty feel better. He had decided to clean out the bamboo corner for his mother, who was really sorry that he had chicken pox and couldn't go on the school picnic. It was a plan that he could always change if he found he wasn't enjoying it.

So that was how Monty came to find the black box. He picked it up. It was dirty, and rusty around the hinges, but that only made it look older and all the more interesting. Monty sat down on the grass and worked around the lid of the box with a stick until he had loosened it a little.

Then he ran to the workshop and found the oilcan. He smeared oil around the hinges and around the edges where he had loosened the rust. At last he felt the lid move, and, after trying again, he wriggled it off. The box was open.

Inside were four lovely big marbles with twisty nets of color winding through the glass. There was a bear carved out of wood, and a little pocketknife with a handle that might have been made of silver. There was a bit of blue glass, worn smooth by the sea and filled with watery sea lights. Last of all there was a necklace . . . a pattern of greeny-blue stones hung on a delicate, dull chain. Monty touched it carefully, and wondered how the box came to be buried in the bamboo corner.

He decided to take it to his father.

"Treasure, treasure!" he shouted, running around the house and into the kitchen where his parents were having a quiet cup of tea.

"What have you got there?" his father asked, taking up the little box and peering into it curiously. His expression changed as he saw the necklace and as Monty told his story.

"If it weren't for the necklace, we needn't worry," his father said at last. "But I think it's probably rather valuable. It looks like turquoise to me . . . turquoise on a silver chain. How on earth did it get there?"

"If we were detectives," Monty said, "we could find out. We could go to the people who lived in this house before us, and ask. . . . But we aren't detectives, and I've got chicken pox."

His father suddenly laughed. "What's the phone for, Monty? It might have been invented just for detectives with chicken pox. I'll start! I'll call Mr. Davis. We bought the house from him, and he might be able to tell us something."

Monty waited by the phone as his father telephoned. He tried to guess from his father's words what Mr. Davis was saying. It was nothing interesting. Mr. Davis knew nothing about boxes of treasure buried in the garden.

Monty's father put down the phone. "He says that the people who lived here while he was renting the house, before we bought it, had only grown-up daughters."

"It's a boy's treasure," said Monty. "All but the necklace."

"I think you're right. Anyway, that family moved down to Victoria. Mr. Davis bought the house from a Miss Dunbar. She's dead now," said Monty's father, frowning.

"Her sisters are alive, though," said Mother unexpectedly. "Mrs. Casely at the Milk Bar is one of them — she might be able to tell us something. She'll be at work this morning."

"Your turn to phone!" said his father, holding out the phone to Mother. "Anyway, you know this Mrs. Casely."

Mrs. Casely had a booming voice, and Monty could hear it clearly when his mother called, coming all the way over the wires from the Milk Bar where she had worked for years.

"Turquoise?" she bellowed. "No, no, nothing like that! No! She had some nice pearls once — well, not real ones, you know, but nice — you couldn't tell the difference. But not turquoise. Well, I don't know! We were there from childhood. Maybe if you were to call Mr. Mills — Horatio Mills, that is — he's still alive. He had the house before my father bought it. He's been around since the year dot."

"What does she mean — the year dot?" asked Monty when his mother had put down the phone.

"She means he's lived around here for a long time," said his father. "Listen, Monty, it's your turn to call. Why should we do all your detective work for you? Let's see, now . . . Mills, H. D. Here's the number. He lives over at Carden, it seems."

Monty took the phone firmly and dialed the number. He heard the distant phone bell going *brrr . . . brrr . . . brrr. . . .* Then a gentle old voice spoke suddenly in his ear. "Hello?"

"Is that Mr. Horatio Mills?" Monty asked.

"Yes!" said the voice, sounding grave and rustly.

Monty told him who he was and where he lived, and explained that he was trying to locate people who had once lived in the house because of something he had found.

"What sort of thing?" asked Mr. Horatio Mills.

"It's something I dug up," said Monty cautiously.

"Indeed!" said Mr. Horatio Mills. "Not a little metal box with marbles in it?"

"And a knife!" said Monty.

"And a turquoise necklace!" said Mr. Horatio Mills.

His voice sounded quite firm and brisk all at once. "I'll come across right away."

"You'd better not," said Monty sadly. "Not unless you've had chicken pox, which is what I've got."

There was a strange sound over the phone: It seemed that Mr. Horatio Mills might be laughing.

"I have had it," he said. "Indeed . . . But I'll tell you about that when I see you. I'll drive over now."

It took twenty minutes for Mr. Horatio Mills to arrive. He drove up in an old car, very clean and shining. Mr. Horatio Mills was rather like his car — very old, but very spruce and well cared for.

He smiled at Monty's parents, and shook hands with Monty. "Mr. Monty Forest, I presume?" he said.

Monty nodded. He felt too excited to speak.

The box was on the table. Mr. Horatio Mills got out his glasses, polished them, and put them on. He examined the box and touched

it with his thin old hands. "Yes . . ." he said at last. "This is the box." He picked up the little pocketknife. "This was mine, once."

"I can see it's a most exciting story," said Mother. "Let me pour you a cup of tea, and you can tell us all about Monty's find." She settled old Mr. Mills in a sunny chair with a cup of tea before he was allowed to begin his story.

"My father built this house," he began. "At that time there were no other houses on this ridge. It stood in the middle of fields and trees. There was a big tree where the garage is now, and a long garden stretching down the slope. My brothers and I played a lot in that big tree. Our favorite game was pirates. We swarmed up and down its branches like a troop of monkeys, pretending we were reefing sails and climbing up the rigging. There were three of us — Thomas, Reginald, and me, Horatio.

"One day, Thomas, who was the eldest and made all the plans, decided that he would bury treasure for us two younger ones to find. We all had to put something into the box. But when we had done this it still looked rather empty, so Thomas did a very naughty thing. He sneaked upstairs to our mother's room and pinched one of her necklaces. It made it seem much more like real pirate treasure, I must admit. Then off he went and hid the box . . . But, as you see, we didn't find it."

"But Thomas would remember where he'd put it," said Monty, puzzled. "Even if you and Reginald couldn't find it — he'd know where it was."

"That's just it!" said Mr. Horatio Mills, clearly enjoying himself. "He *didn't* remember. We began our search by climbing up the big tree. We thought he might have hidden it there. Thomas climbed up with us — and he slipped, and fell. He had what is called concussion. We were all very worried about him for a day or two, but he got better after that. The only thing was . . . he couldn't remember one single thing about the day of his accident. So we just didn't know where he had hidden the treasure, and though we searched and searched, we never found it."

"It was in the bamboo corner under the fence," Monty said.

"So!" said Mr. Horatio Mills, and nodded his head. "The bamboo had just been planted then. And, you must remember, there was a lot more land and garden to search in those days. How funny that another boy should have found it after all these years! I'll take the necklace back for my little granddaughter, if you don't mind, but I'd like you to have the rest of the treasure, Monty. It isn't a very valuable or exciting treasure, but it is truly old, and it was truly buried and lost."

Monty drew a deep breath. "I think it's a wonderful treasure," he said. "It seems special somehow, because there were boys who buried it all those years ago — just the same sort of treasure I might bury myself, if I had to." He looked around at his mother and father, then back to Mr. Horatio Mills. "And it seems funny to think I was sad about missing the school treasure hunt today — and then found another treasure here, all through having chicken pox! Golly, Mr. Mills, I hope you don't catch it!"

Mr. Horatio Mills smiled. "I don't expect I will. I've already had it. In fact" — and his eyes twinkled behind his glasses — "it was because Thomas, Reginald, and I had chicken pox that we were at home that sunny day all those years ago when Thomas buried the treasure!"

Mrs. Bartelmy's Pet

High on a hill in her pointed house lived fierce little Mrs. Bartelmy, who had once been a pirate queen. She lived there on her own with her gold earrings and wooden leg, and a box of treasure buried in her garden under the sunflowers.

Though she was fierce, Mrs. Bartelmy often felt lonely. She was used to having lots of adventures. She was used to the cheerful,

wicked conversation of pirates. Now she lived on her own, she often wished for someone to talk to.

I could get a cat, thought Mrs. Bartelmy, but they are tame, sleepy animals. I am such a fierce old woman, my cat would probably be scared of me. I wish I had been only a granny and not a pirate queen. Then a cat would have loved me.

Mrs. Bartelmy was fond of sunflowers. She planted them all around her house. They grew so tall, they almost hid the roof. One day, when Mrs. Bartelmy was digging among them, she found the biggest cat she had ever seen sleeping there. It was a yellow cat with a small waist and tufted tail, and Mrs. Bartelmy liked it at once. It had a golden mane around its face that reminded her of sunflowers. It yawned and showed its red mouth and white teeth. Then it smiled at Mrs. Bartelmy.

Mrs. Bartelmy gave it a big bowl of milk and a string of sausages. The cat lapped the milk. It ate all the sausages and growled fiercely.

"That's the boy!" said Mrs. Bartelmy. "I like a chap who enjoys his food. You're fierce enough for me, and I'm fierce enough for you. We'll get along together like a couple of jolly shipmates."

At that moment the gate squeaked. Mrs. Bartelmy looked up to see who was coming. Four men with huge nets and a fat man with a whip were walking up the path.

"We are circus men looking for our lion," said one of the men.

"The wicked, ungrateful animal has run away," said the fat man. "I am Signor Rosetta, the lion tamer." He cracked his whip.

At the sound of the whip the big yellow cat leaped out, roaring furiously. Mrs. Bartelmy's big cat was a lion!

"You aren't to chase this lion," said Mrs. Bartelmy. "He's a half-fierce, half-friendly lion, and he's my shipmate."

"Well, you could have him," said Signor Rosetta, "but we need him for the circus, and we haven't got enough money to buy another lion."

"Is that your only worry?" exclaimed Mrs. Bartelmy. She took the spade to a secret corner of her sunflower garden and dug up her chest of pirate treasure. She gave the lion tamer two handfuls of diamonds and Indian rubies.

"Is this enough to buy him?" she asked.

The lion tamer was delighted.

"It is enough to hire a whole troupe of clowns. Ours will be the funniest circus in the world!" he cried.

And so he went away, and the men with the nets went with him.

"That's that," said Mrs. Bartelmy. Once the lion tamer, his whip, and his nets were gone, the lion became gentle again and smiled at Mrs. Bartelmy. It had flowers in its mane and smelled of new hay.

"Well, I never thought to find a cat so much to my liking," said Mrs. Bartelmy. "I won't have to worry about scaring it when I feel fierce. And it matches my sunflowers too."

The lion and Mrs. Bartelmy lived happily ever after. Often I have

passed them sitting on the doorstep of their pointed house among the sunflowers, singing with all their might:

Oh, there was an old woman
who lived on her own
In a little house made from a smooth
white bone.
And she sat at her door with a
barrel of beer,
And a bright gold ring in her old
brown ear.
And folk who passed by her
they always agreed,
That's a queer little,
wry little,
fierce little,
spry little,
Utterly strange little
woman indeed!

The Witch-Dog

There was once a mother whose children had all grown up and were either away at work or married. This mother now had nothing to do but tidy her already tidy house and weed her neat garden. She did not find this very interesting. So, one day, this mother — her name was Mrs. Rose — said to her husband, "My dear, I find life a little slow now, with the children all being away. I think I'll join a club, or take a class in something."

"That's a good idea," said Mr. Rose. "How about bowling?" (He bowled himself, you see.)

"Well, no, I don't fancy that," said Mrs. Rose. "I'd never be good enough to play with *you*, my dear. No, I've had something in mind for a day or two: I think I'll learn to be a witch. I saw in the paper that there are classes in witchcraft at night school."

"They certainly have some unusual classes at night school these days," said Mr. Rose. "Just as you like, my dear. I'm sure you will enjoy it."

Mrs. Rose turned out to be very good at witchcraft. While other pupils were struggling to pull rabbits out of hats, Mrs. Rose was able to pull out ribbons, sparrows, buttercups and daisies, little silver fish, frogs, dragonflies, and poems written in gold on pink paper. She found it easy. The Head Witch was pleased.

"My dear Witch Rose," she said, "you are doing excellently — *excellently*. You may come and dance at our Witch Dance as soon as you have mastered your broomstick technique." Mrs. Rose was delighted — it was a special honor to be allowed to dance in a Witch Dance, and she knew she was the only one in the class to be invited. She worked hard with her broomstick. First she learned to balance and then to soar, and soon she was soaring and swooping like a cinder in the wind.

"Well, Witch Rose," said the Head Witch, "you're a most creditable pupil. Next Friday you may come to our Witch Dance and we'll be pleased to have you. You must make yourself a cloak and hat and get yourself a cat, too, if you don't have one already."

Mrs. Rose suddenly looked very dismayed.

"A cat!" she exclaimed. But the Head Witch had whisked off hastily to talk to some other pupil not nearly as clever as Mrs. Rose.

"A cat!" muttered Mrs. Rose, for there was something she hadn't told the Head Witch — something she hadn't even thought about, something that meant, perhaps, that she could never ever be a true witch and dance at the Witch Dances.

"What am I going to do?" she cried to Mr. Rose. "Cat's fur makes me sneeze my head off. I won't be able to go, and I would like to, having gotten so far. But even a kitten makes me sneeze."

"Get a dog instead," suggested Mr. Rose. "A small portable dog — one that will fit onto the end of a broomstick. I know it's not usual, but there we are — and dogs don't make you sneeze."

"Oh, do you think a dog would do instead?" Mrs. Rose said. "I wonder. . . . That's a good idea of yours, Tom. I'll think about it." She didn't have to think long, for, by a curious coincidence, the first thing she saw when she went out to the garden the next morning was a funny little lost dog — just the sort that could fit on the end of a broomstick. He had no collar but he had a cheerful expression and Mrs. Rose liked him at once. She liked his silvery gray coat, which was shaggy and hung down almost to his feet, and she liked his merry ears which stuck up straight into the air and then changed their minds and hung down at the tips.

"Would you like to be a witch-dog?" Mrs. Rose asked him, and he wriggled his nose in a dog grin and wagged his tail. "Very well," said Mrs. Rose, "you shall be, and I will call you 'Nightshade.' That's a good witch-name, and ought to please the witches."

On Saturday night Mrs. Rose put on her hat and cloak and tucked her wand into her belt. She climbed onto her broomstick. Nightshade hopped on behind as if he had been born to it. A

moment later they were up in the air, Mrs. Rose pointing her broomstick in the direction of Miller's Hill.

Already the bare place at the top of Miller's Hill was bustling and rustling with witches — lots of witches. They had lit a huge fire and were standing around it, some with cats and some with solemn owls. When Mrs. Rose and Nightshade glided down among them they were quiet enough, except for the usual witch noises such as muttering, cackling, and wicked screaming. But in the next moment there was scratching and scrambling and shouting, for, at

the sight of Nightshade, the cats put out their claws, puffed up their fur, and shot off into the shadows and up trees. The owls took off in a whirl of angry feathers.

The Head Witch bore down furiously on Mrs. Rose and Nightshade. "What do you think you are up to, Witch Rose? Really, my dear, a witch can be wicked — but never, never stupid! Why are you bringing a daylight animal like a dog to our festivities?"

"Well," said Mrs. Rose, "the fact is, cats make me sneeze. I like cats, but they make me sneeze terribly." The Head Witch was silent with amazement. Mrs. Rose went on quickly, "I'm sure Nightshade will make a splendid witch-dog. There's a lot to him, Head Witch, and once the cats get used to him . . ."

The Head Witch was frowning and about to interrupt, when a surprising and terrible thing happened, distracting her attention from Mrs. Rose. A large toad, as big as a cat, hopped, croaking furiously, into the circle of witches. Their squeaking, squealing, and cackling stopped and they stared long and hard at the toad. Even Mrs. Rose, without any practice, could see that it was no ordinary toad, but an enchanted witch.

"Goodness gracious, it's Smudge — Witch Smudge!" cried the Head Witch. "I must see what's wrong. I'll deal with your problem later, Witch Rose, but I'm afraid it won't do." She turned to the toad. "Smudge, what are you doing here in that condition? You can speak freely. You are among friends. Or is this a joke?"

The toad croaked indignantly.

"What?" said the Head Witch. "Not really! Smudge, you *are* a fool!"

She turned and spoke to the other witches. "Witch Smudge has behaved imprudently and has been enchanted by an enchanter for a month. I must say he must be one of the old-fashioned sort of enchanters to turn her into a toad — but he certainly made a good job of it, and there's nothing we can do about it. I only wish he'd turned her into a pound of sausages. She deserves it."

A great groaning and moaning and howling burst forth from the leathery throats of the witches and rose up to the moon.

"The fact is," the Head Witch murmured to Mrs. Rose, "Witch Smudge is one of the most amusing and wicked witches in our group. She plays the funniest, wickedest witch-music. It's a delight to dance our circles to her tunes. . . . And now she's got herself turned into a toad, the selfish creature. We've no other musician. I don't see what we are going to do."

Upon hearing this, Mrs. Rose's dog, Nightshade, sat back on his hind legs and from under his long silvery coat he whipped out a little violin — a little violin made of silvery wood with three green strings and one golden one. He snatched a twig of goldenrod, and drew it over the strings, which played a few notes of the maddest, funniest, wickedest witch-music that you ever heard.

The cats slid down from the trees and the owls came circling out of the night. The witches began to jig and kick, showing their red-and-black striped stockings. Then Nightshade played even harder, and oh, how those witches whirled and swirled! The owls spun and spiraled in the night air, the cats crouched and punched and boxed each other with delight in the shadows, while the music grew fiercer and faster and more piercing still. When at last it stopped, all the witches, owls, and cats fell in a heap on the top of Miller's Hill, legs kicking out in all directions. The Head Witch disentangled herself, biting somebody's leg as she did so, and felt around among the cats and owls and the other witches until she found Mrs. Rose, who had been dancing with the best of them. They shook hands warmly.

"That was no ordinary music," said the Head Witch. "And you are no ordinary witch, Witch Rose. You can keep your dog, and we'll give him the title of Witch-Cat Extraordinary."

So that is why, whenever the witches meet on Miller's Hill for their wicked frolics, Mrs. Rose always dances among them — one of the most respected witches to come out of night school. And, playing the wild, shrill music on his fiddle, Nightshade dances too — the first dog ever to become a witch-cat.

The Breakfast Bird

"Look!" said Johnny. "Look at Cathie's toast!"

Everyone looked at Cathie's toast.

"Oh, Cathie!" said Mother. "You've done it again. There is honey everywhere!"

There was honey all over Cathie's toast. There was honey all over Cathie's plate. There was honey all over Cathie's face.

"You have even got it on the tablecloth," said Mother.

"Well, I like honey," said Cathie. "I like *plenty* of honey."

"You are a greedy honey bear," said Mother. "Most of that honey will be wasted."

"Not if I lick my plate out in the kitchen," replied Cathie. "It won't be wasted then."

"Bad manners, though!" said Mack, the eldest of the children.

"It isn't bad manners out in the kitchen," argued Johnny. "Licking plates is only bad manners at the table."

This was a family rule.

"As long as she doesn't try to lick the tablecloth," Mack answered in a grunty voice. Things began to quiet down. Then Johnny began again.

"Mom, you know Mr. Cooney's budgie has hatched out babies."

"No. How should I know?" asked Mother. "You've only told me twenty times already." She was trying to scrape honey off the tablecloth as she spoke.

"Well, can't I have one? Please, *please*!" begged Johnny. "I'd teach it to talk and perch on my finger. Mr. Cooney's budgie perches on his finger."

"Yes, you might teach it to perch," said Mother, "but would you remember to give it fresh water? Would you clean out its cage and make sure it had plenty of seed every day? I don't think you would."

"Yes, I would!" Johnny cried quickly, his eyes blue and startled in his freckled face. "I'd help in the garden too. Budgies like something fresh and green every day."

Mother laughed.

"I'll tell you what . . ." she said at last. "Today, Cathie's Play Center group finishes for the holidays. The mothers have to take the pets home and feed and look after them until the Play Center begins again. Shall I offer to bring the budgie home? Then we can just see how good you are at looking after a budgie."

"He's a nice budgie," called Cathie. "His name is Nippy because he tries to bite our fingers."

"If he bit your finger," said Mack, "he'd get a beakful of honey. His beak would be stuck up for hours."

When Johnny came home from school the next day his mother said, "There's a visitor in the living room."

"Yes," Cathie cried like a squeaky echo, "there's a green visitor sitting on the table."

The green visitor was Nippy, the Play Center budgie.

Johnny wanted a blue budgie, not a green one.

He went up to the Play Center cage and looked at Nippy.

Nippy looked back at Johnny from little black eyes. Nippy looked like a small round-shouldered pirate. He looked like a goblin in a green shawl. He shuffled along his perch — six steps left, six steps right. Then he hooked his beak over the wire of the cage, crawled up the wire, and hung upside down on the roof.

"Will he sit on my finger?" asked Johnny.

"Well, he's very tame," said Mother, "but I don't want you to open the big door of his cage at all. Remember, he isn't ours. It would be a great pity to lose him."

Every morning Johnny gave Nippy fresh water. Every morning Johnny checked Nippy's birdseed.

"Johnny! Johnny!" called Mother. "Where have you gotten to?"

"I'm just getting Nippy some sow thistle," came Johnny's voice from a weedy part of the garden.

"Hey, Johnny, where are you?" shouted Mack.

"Cutting a piece of apple for Nippy," answered Johnny from the kitchen.

Every three days Johnny cleaned out Nippy's cage. He wanted to show his mother just how well he could look after a budgie.

"Johnny, where are you?" cried Cathie from the hall.

"Talking to Nippy!" Johnny called back. "I don't want him to be lonely while he's on vacation."

"I'm glad the Play Center pet isn't an owl," remarked Father. "We'd have Johnny up all night catching mice for it."

The holidays went by quickly.

"You've taken such good care of Nippy, Johnny, that I think we could let you have a blue budgie," his mother said. "We'll go and see Mr. Cooney about it tomorrow."

The first day of the new school term came around.

Johnny was trying to keep his clean first-morning-of-school clothes tidy and give Nippy fresh seed. Nippy ran backward and forward on his perch. His feet were wrinkled and gray, with two claws curling forward and two toes curling back. Once, Mr. Cooney had let Johnny put his hand into the Cooney budgie's cage, and a blue Cooney budgie had settled on his finger. Its feet, which looked horny and cold, were smooth and warm. It had shuffled and bobbed and winked at Johnny.

Suddenly he wanted, very much, to feel those smooth warm feet again.

There was no one in the room but Cathie, and she was not watching him. Instead she was getting her breakfast ready, spreading a great spoonful of honey on her toast. It took only a moment to open the big door of the cage. Johnny slid his hand in and pressed a clean first-morning-of-school finger against Nippy's green chest. Nippy stepped onto Johnny's finger. His gray feet were just as small and warm as Johnny expected them to be.

Slowly Nippy walked over Johnny's hand, moving sideways, with his head tilted. Then, he did a quick little dance, and before Johnny knew what was happening, Nippy had slid across his wrist and out of the cage door. His wings fluttered wildly. Nippy was flying around and around the room, and there was nothing Johnny could do but stand and stare. Cathie stared too. Two pairs of round blue eyes followed the green budgie around and around and around. At last, Nippy landed on the cord of the electric light. He hung there staring back at them. It was terrible. In another moment Johnny knew their mother would come in. She would know that Johnny had opened the big door of the Play Center cage

and had let Nippy out. There would be no blue Cooney budgie for Johnny unless Nippy could be caught and returned to his cage before Play Center time.

Nippy took off again, whirring around the room. He flew lower this time and settled on the curtain rod.

"Climb on a chair and catch him," breathed Cathie. Johnny scrambled onto a chair, but before his hand was anywhere near Nippy, off Nippy flew, around and around and around. His wings made a busy breathing sound in the still room. Johnny began to run backward and forward beneath him. Nippy flew lower and lower and lower, as if his wings were getting tired. He landed on the table.

"Johnny!" cried Cathie. Nippy had landed on her piece of toast.

The toast was thickly spread with honey. Nippy could not get his feet out of it.

In a moment Johnny had caught him again. Holding him very gently he wiped Nippy's tiny honey-covered feet with his clean first-morning-of-school handkerchief. When most of the honey was off he slipped the little bird back into the Play Center cage.

"Gosh!" mumbled Cathie, staring at her toast. "I don't think this toast is good anymore. I thought it was salt you had to put on the tail for catching birds."

"Honey on the feet is better," said Johnny, beginning to grin again, though the grin felt stiff as if it were a new one he was wearing for the first time.

"Should we tell?" asked Cathie.

"If anyone asks, we have to tell," Johnny answered carefully.

Cathie nodded to herself.

"No one will ask," she murmured, and began licking her sticky fingers.

The door opened and their mother came in.

"Haven't you finished yet?" she cried.

"I have really," said Cathie. "The trouble was—too much toast."

"Put it in the hens' dish in the kitchen," said Mother. "The hens will love it."

"They'd better not stand on it," said Cathie very seriously.

A minute later they were ready to go. Mother and Cathie were off to the Play Center. Mack and Johnny were off to school. Mother carried Nippy in his Play Center cage. Just as they were about to go, Nippy looked through the bars of his cage at Johnny.

"Johnny!" he shouted, "Johnny! Johnny! Johnny! Where are you?"

"Oh!" gasped Johnny. "He called me. He called my name."

"Oh dear!" said Mother. "Just what do we do now?"

For Johnny suddenly knew that he did not want a blue Cooney budgie after all. He wanted Nippy, that wicked green Nippy who could call his name. Mother seemed to understand this, for she smiled and then began to laugh a little bit.

"Off to school," she said. "We'll talk about it after school."

When Johnny came home that afternoon a voice shouted at him as soon as he came into the room.

"Johnny! Johnny! Where's Johnny?"

Nippy was in his usual place, as green and dancing as ever. However, he had a new cage, even larger than the Play Center one, with a swing and two seed boxes.

His feet were covered in seed husks.

"He's wearing boots," said Cathie. Her round blue eyes were

smiling. "Mom bought a blue Cooney budgie for the Play Center, so we are allowed to keep Nippy for always. Aren't you pleased?"

"Of course I am," Johnny answered. "He is the one I wanted after all."

"He can come out of his cage and fly around the room now that he's a member of the family," Cathie went on.

"If we can work out how to catch him again," said Mother, "though he is so tame he will usually go back to his cage himself after a while."

"No need to worry, anyway, Mom," said Johnny, beginning to laugh. "Cathie could catch him in her breakfast bird trap."

And with Nippy listening and shouting encouragement, Johnny and Cathie began to tell their mother about the honey-and-budgie-breakfast adventure.

Teddy and the Witches

Once there were three witches flying over the world and looking down at it from their broomsticks. One had white hair, one had black hair, and one had hair like wild bright flame, and all three had gleaming golden eyes. . . . They were looking for mischief to do.

At last they came to a long, green valley which they had never seen before in all their magic lives, and their eyes shone as they looked at the snug-as-a-bug-in-a-rug farms and the soft, smudgy shadows in the creases of the hills.

"Here," they said to each other, "is a wonderful place for some mischief." And they smiled. . . .

The first witch pointed her finger. *Tweedle dee!* All the pigs grew silver wings and flew up into the trees with the magpies.

The second witch clapped her hands and all the hens turned into parrots and cockatoos — scarlet and green, white and yellow — and filled the air with their merry screechings.

But the third witch, the redheaded one, just blinked her golden eyes and all the cows became elephants — and elephants eat a lot of grass and are very hard to milk.

Then the witches sat back to enjoy the mischief, like wasps around a honey pot.

Now, in this valley lived a small boy called Teddy. He had brown eyes, he was always hungry, and his head was full of deep, secret ways of thinking. And when he went out the next morning and found the hen coop full of parrots and cockatoos, he thought to himself, Witches! And when he saw the next-door-farmer's fields

full of large gray crumpled-looking elephants, he thought to himself, Witches! And then when he heard the pigs squealing in the trees, he thought, It's those witches again. I must do something about them.

And so Teddy sat down with a ball of string and some pieces of rope and worked at a secret thing. His mother walked by him to the clothesline.

"What are you making, little Teddy?" she asked. "Is it a net of some kind?"

"It isn't a net," Teddy answered. "It's called 'Little Hand Snatching at the Stars.'"

His mother smiled and went on her way. She did not know that 'Little Hand Snatching at the Stars' was part of a witch trap.

It was late in the afternoon when the witch trap was finished. Teddy hung it between two tall pine trees, and on the ground underneath the trap he put some pieces of a broken mirror, two shining tin-can lids, and some teaspoons which he had taken from the drawer when his mother wasn't looking. The idea was that the witches would see some bright things shining, and would fly down to see what they were. And then they would be caught in the trap. . . .

56

Sure enough, next morning, when Teddy looked out of the window, he saw something like a flame caught beneath the pine trees. There, very beautiful and glowing, was the youngest witch — the redheaded one — like a fly in a spider's web. Down on the ground lay her pointed hat, her cloak, and her broomstick.

Teddy ran out into the garden.

"Hello, little fellow," she said very sweetly to Teddy. "Could you pass me my broomstick and hat, please?"

Teddy knew that a witch's magic lies in her hat and broomstick. He did not give them to her, but took them inside and hid them in his closet behind the raincoats. Then he took a jump rope and went out to the witch again. After he had set her free from the witch trap, Teddy tied the jump rope around her ankles.

"What are you going to do with me?" she asked, so sweetly that it was hard to believe she would do any mischief. But in the next field Teddy could see great bare patches eaten by elephants that had once been cows.

"During the day," he said, "you will be able to help my mother. But at night I will tie you up to the hen house. If it rains, you can get inside." (This was not at all cruel as witches are used to perching at night.)

"But I don't like parrots," said the witch, looking at the brightly colored hen coop.

"You should have thought of that before," Teddy answered.

"Well, I won't be here long, anyway," said the witch, with a toss of her wild red hair. "My sisters will set me free very quickly and you will be sorry you ever thought of making a witch trap."

Teddy's mother was surprised when he brought the witch inside, but she listened to his story and said that the witch might dry the breakfast dishes. At first the witch was sulky and cross but, as the morning passed, she grew more cheerful. Then, just before lunch, the grocer's van drove up and the young driver got out to bring in the box of groceries that Teddy's mother had ordered.

It was plain that the witch was very pleased with his black curly hair and merry eyes.

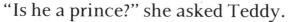

"Is he a prince?" she asked Teddy.

"No, he's the grocer's man," Teddy answered.

"How are you, young fellow?" the grocer's man said to Teddy as he came in. He looked at the witch. It was plain that he was very pleased with her wild red hair and golden eyes. After he had talked for a while he went off — leaving a dozen eggs that should have gone to somebody else. After this the witch seemed almost happy.

Before he went to bed that night Teddy pinned a spray of fern to his pajamas. He had read somewhere that it was a good protection against witch spells. It was just as well he did, for in the night there was more witch trouble. . . .

Teddy had fallen asleep when, suddenly, his bed shook itself and then flew out of the window. Outside, the two witches screamed at him.

"Give us back our sister," they screeched. They flew at him, making claws with their long fingers. "Give us back our sister or you will go for a wild ride."

Teddy was not afraid. He answered, "First you must take the magic off the valley and give us back our cows and hens."

"Never, never!" yelled the witches. They tried to magic Teddy, but the spells bounced back with a twanging sound. This was because of the fern Teddy was wearing.

58

"Well," said the white-haired witch, "we may not be able to touch you, but we can change your bed."

Then Teddy's bed began to buck and kick, to slide and glide, to bumble and stumble, to creep and leap, and to highstep and lowstep, until Teddy felt quite giddy.

"Will you set her free?" the witches screamed. (They could not rescue her themselves without her broomstick and hat and cloak, and of course they did not know where Teddy had hidden them.)

"No, of course I won't," Teddy answered.

Then his bed became a wild horse, with furious wings and hooves of thunder, and it raced wildly up and down the valley. But Teddy

held on tightly with his knees, and twisted his hands in its mane — and after a while the horse stood still.

Then the bed became a fiery dragon which hissed and twisted to get at Teddy, but he curled up small between the dragon's wings, and its claws could not reach him. And so, in its turn, the dragon grew still.

And then the bed became a great wind, and it tossed Teddy like thistledown. But he lay limp in the wind and thought happy thoughts, and pretended he was bouncing on his bed at home.

At last the white-haired witch said, "That was just my sister's magic. I'm going to send you around the world!" She said something

to the bed which at once set off at a terrific speed and flew all the way around the world. But Teddy sat in the middle of his bed and sang nursery rhymes and took no notice at all of the hot or the cold, or the green or the gold, or the pounding, bounding sea. At last the bed came home again, and as it did so, there was the sound of breaking violin strings. The witches had taken their spells off the valley. Down from the trees floated the pigs. They shook free their silver wings which fluttered off to another place. Where they went, I can't tell you at all. And the parrots and cockatoos — scarlet and green, white and yellow — became clucking, scratching hens again.

Then the oldest witch — the white-haired one — said to Teddy, "The mischief is undone, as far as we can undo it. Our sister must undo her own spell, and turn the elephants back to cows." With that they flew away into the new morning that was poking its bright face over the hills.

When he got up, Teddy went into the kitchen. The witch was putting apples on the stove to stew for breakfast. She wore one of his mother's aprons, and her long red hair hung in a pigtail down her back.

"Your sisters have taken off their magic," Teddy told her. "And if you turn the elephants back to cows I will give you back your broomstick, cloak, and hat."

"My sisters?" said the witch. "My broomstick? Oh yes, that's right. I'm a witch! I had forgotten." She waved her hand and there

was the sound of a bell note, faint, far away, and rather sad. "There now, the magic is gone."

"Well, thank you," Teddy answered. "I'll go and get your broomstick."

"Keep it yourself," said the witch. "I don't want it. I like it here. I'm tired of being a witch. Besides, tonight I'm going out with the grocer's man."

"Really, I can't think what I'd do without her," said Teddy's mother. "She is such a help to me. It's just like magic."

The witch looked pleased.

Teddy thought for a while. "Can I really have your hat and broomstick?" he asked, at last.

"You might as well," she answered, "for I don't want them."

The people in the valley had just gotten over the shock of finding their pigs, hens, and cows had come back to them, when they were surprised to see Teddy on a broomstick and wearing a high steeple hat, flying overhead.

"There's that Teddy!" they said to each other. "What will he be up to next?"

The broomstick flicked a bit as if it were laughing. But Teddy pointed upward, and it flew higher and higher, like a little bird trying to reach the sun. Up into the blue, blue air it went, and there Teddy soared and swooped like a small wind, happy among the clouds.

The Boy Who Went Looking for a Friend

One day, a little boy called Sam said to his mother, "I am lonely. Where can I find a friend?"

His mother said, "Behind our house is a field. It is filled with grass and red poppies and cornflowers. There are stalks of wild wheat. There are big brown-and-yellow butterflies. Go into the field, Sam. Perhaps you will find a friend there."

The little boy went into the field. Among the poppies and the grass he met a tiger. The tiger was as yellow as sunshine. His coat

was streaked with dark stripes. He had a very long twitching tail.

"Hello, Tiger," said Sam.

"Hello, Sam," said the tiger. He yawned a tiger yawn. His teeth looked very white.

"Are you the sort of tiger that eats boys?" asked Sam.

"No!" said the tiger. "I only eat sandwiches. I have some sandwiches in this paper bag. Would you like some?" Sam and the tiger had a picnic on the grass. Then they played hide-and-seek all over the field. They hid up in trees and behind trees, and made long secret tunnels through the grass. They had a lot of fun. But at sunset the tiger said, "I must be going now."

"Will you come back?" asked Sam.

"Perhaps I will," said the tiger. "Or perhaps I won't," and off he went, waving his tail.

Next day Sam said to his mother, "I am lonely — where can I find a friend?"

His mother said, "You know that tree down at the bottom of our

garden? It is the tallest tree in the world. Its branches are so wide that sixteen wise monkeys could dance on them and there would still be room for you. You could put a table and chairs on its branches and eat your lunch there. Go to the tall tree, little Sam. You may find friends there."

Off went Sam to the tall tree. There, on its branches, danced sixteen clever monkeys.

"Hello, you monkeys!" called Sam. "Can I climb up and dance with you?"

The monkeys made themselves into a long monkey-ladder and Sam climbed up it into the branches. On a big branch of the tree was a table and seventeen chairs. Sam and the monkeys sat down to eat. They ate pancakes and pineapple, sausages and straw-berries. They drank raspberry juice out of tall clear glasses. Then they put on funny hats and laughed and sang. However, just as they were all having a lovely time, the sun set. The monkeys started to climb the tree. They climbed much faster than Sam could.

"Where are you going to, monkeys?" he called.

"Higher up, higher up," the monkeys squealed.

"Will you come back tomorrow?" asked Sam.

"Perhaps," said the monkeys, "or perhaps not." And off they went, swinging by their tails.

Next day Sam said to his mother, "I am lonely. Where can I find a friend?"

"Outside our gate," said his mother, "is a long road. It leads from a big town to a small town. It is dusty and gray. Along that road go all sorts of people. Some are in cars, some are on horses, some are on bicycles. Sometimes nobody goes by for a long time. But listen . . . I hear music on the road. Run and see, little Sam! It might be a friend."

Sam heard the music and ran down to the gate.

"*Ta-ra-ra-ra!*" went a trumpet. "*Rat-a-plan-plan!*" went a drum. A circus was coming by. There were white horses and black horses. There were lions and elephants. There were bags of peanuts and popcorn and hundreds of balloons. Best of all, there was Jimmy, the funny clown. The circus stopped.

"Here is Sam!" said Jimmy. "Let's show him the circus." The juggler juggled plates and cups and balls and balloons for Sam. He did not drop one. The clowns danced. A lovely fairy girl rode her white horse. She stood on its back, light as a feather, and did not fall off once. The men on the flying trapeze swung to and fro and tossed and turned in the air. Sam clapped and shouted. Most of all he laughed at Jimmy, the funny clown, riding his donkey backward. Soon, the sun began to set. The circus packed up and set off down the road.

"Where are you going?" called Sam.

"Farther on! Farther on!" called Jimmy, the funniest clown of all, riding his donkey backward.

"Will you ever come back?" asked Sam.

"Perhaps we will, or perhaps we won't," cried Jimmy. And off they went around a bend in the road.

The next day Sam was too sad to ask his mother where he could find a friend.

All my friends go away, he thought. They all go to places where I can't go. He went down to the river and sat with his feet in the watercress. Then around a bend in the river came a boat with a blue sail. As it reached Sam, it stopped by the watercress, and a boy leaped out. He was just Sam's size of boy, with an ordinary brown face and brown hair.

"Hello!" he said. "I didn't know you lived here. My name is Philip. What's your name?"

"Sam!" said Sam.

"Get in my boat and we will sail some more," said Philip. "Here's a life preserver that will fit you." They sailed all afternoon. Up and down the riverbank they went, watching the fish in the clear green water. They saw wild ducks swimming, and cows coming down to drink. They saw a bright pheasant in the long grass. All the time they talked and made up stories. It was the best day of all. When it was sunset Philip said, "We must go home now or our mothers will start looking for us. May I come and play with you tomorrow, Sam? You are a good sort of friend to share my boat with me."

"Of course," said Sam, very pleased. "We've had a good time, haven't we?"

"Tomorrow will be even better," said Philip.

Sam went home and said to his mother, "I've got a friend, Mother, and it isn't a tiger, and it isn't monkeys, and it isn't a circus. It's a boy called Philip."

"That's good," said his mother. "Tigers are good friends for tigers. Monkeys are good friends for monkeys, and a circus is everybody's friend, but a boy is the best friend for a boy."

"I didn't have to ask him to come and play tomorrow. He asked *me*," said Sam.

"He sounds the best sort of friend, then," said Sam's mother.

"He wasn't in a field or up a tree or coming down the road," said Sam. "I met him by the river."

"Ah, now," said Sam's mother, "the river brings all things to those who wait."

Patrick Comes to School

"Graham," said the teacher, "will you look after Patrick at recess? Remember, he is new to the school and has no friends here yet."

There were lots of things Graham would rather have done, but he had to smile and say, "Yes, Mr. Porter."

Behind him Harry Biggs gave his funny, grunting laugh and whispered, "Nursey-nursey Graham." But Mr. Porter was watching, so Graham could not say anything back.

Patrick was a little shrimp of a boy with red hair — not just carroty or ginger — a sort of fiery red. There were freckles all over his face, crowded like people on a five o'clock bus, jostling and pushing to get the best places. In fact, Graham thought, Patrick probably had more freckles than face. As well as red hair and freckles, Patrick had a tilted nose and eyes so blue and bright that he looked all the time as if he'd just been given a specially good Christmas present. He seemed cheerful, which was something, but he was a skinny, short little fellow, not likely to be much good at sports, or at looking after himself in a fight.

Just my luck to get stuck with a new boy! thought Graham.

At recess he took Patrick around and showed him the football field and the equipment shed. Graham's friend, Len, came along too. Len and Graham were very polite to Patrick, and he was very polite back, but it wasn't much fun really. Every now and then Len and Graham would look at each other over Patrick's head. It was easy to do, because he was so small. "Gosh, what a nuisance!" the looks said, meaning Patrick.

Just before the bell rang, Harry Biggs came up with three other boys. Harry Biggs was big, and the three other boys were even bigger, and came from a senior class.

"Hello, here's the new boy out with his nurse," said Harry. "What's your name, new boy?"

Graham felt he ought to do something to protect little Patrick, but Patrick spoke out quite boldly and said, "Patrick Fingall O'Donnell." So that was all right.

Harry Biggs frowned at the name. "Now don't be too smart!" he said. "We tear cheeky little kids apart in this school, don't we?" He nudged the other boys, who grinned and shuffled. "Where do you live, O'Donnell?"

Then Patrick said a funny thing. "I live in a house among the trees, and we have a golden bird sitting on our gate."

He clearly wasn't joking. He spoke carefully as if he were asking Harry Biggs a difficult riddle. He sounded as if, in a minute, he might be laughing at Harry Biggs. Harry Biggs must have thought so too, because he frowned even harder and said, "Remember what I told you, and don't be too clever. Now listen . . . What does your father do?"

"Cut it out, Harry," said Graham quickly. "Pick on someone your own size."

"I'm not hurting him, Nursey!" exclaimed Harry. "Go on, Ginger, what does he do for a living?"

Patrick answered quickly, almost as if he were reciting a poem.

"My father wears clothes with gold all over them," said Patrick. "In the morning he says to the men, 'I'll have a look at my elephants this morning,' and he goes and looks at his elephants.

When they see him coming, the elephants wave their trunks at him. He can ride the elephants all day if he wants to, but mostly he is too busy keeping the lions and monkeys happy."

Harry Biggs stared at Patrick with his eyes popping out of his head.

"Who do you think you're kidding?" he said at last. "Are you making out your dad's a king or something? Nobody wears clothes with gold on them."

"My father does!" said Patrick. "Wears them every day!" He thought for a moment. "Lions and tigers purr when they see my father coming to visit them," he added.

"Does he work in a circus?" asked one of the other boys.

"No!" said Patrick. "We'd live in a caravan then, not a house with a golden bird at the gate." Once again Graham felt that Patrick was turning his answers into riddles.

Before anyone could say any more, the bell rang to go back into school.

"Gee, you'll hear all about that!" Len said to Patrick. "Why did you tell him all that stuff?"

"It's true," Patrick said. "He asked me, and it's true."

"He'll think you were pulling his leg," Graham said. "Anyway, it couldn't be true."

"It *is* true," said Patrick, "and it isn't pulling his leg to say what's true, is it?"

"Well, I don't know," Graham muttered to Len. "It doesn't sound very true to me."

Of course, Harry Biggs and the other boys spread the story around the school.

Several children came up to Patrick and asked, "Hey, are all the things your father wears pure gold?"

"Not all," said Patrick. "But quite a lot."

Then the children would laugh and pretend to faint with laughing.

"Hey, Ginger!" called Harry Biggs. "How are all the elephants?"

"All right, thank you," Patrick would reply politely. Once, he added, "We've got a monkey too, at present, and he looks just like you." But he only said it once, because Harry Biggs pulled his hair and twisted his ears. Patrick's ears were nearly as red as his hair.

"Serves you right for showing off," said Graham.

"Well, I might have been showing off a bit," Patrick admitted. "It's hard not to sometimes."

Yet, although they teased him, slowly children came to like Patrick. Graham liked him a lot. He was so good-tempered and full of jokes. Even when someone was laughing at him, he laughed too. The only thing that worried Graham was the feeling that Patrick was laughing at some secret joke.

"Don't you get sick of being teased?" he asked.

"Well, sometimes I feel I've had enough," Patrick said, "but mostly I don't mind. Anyhow, what I said was true, and that's all there is to say."

"I'd hate to be teased so much," Graham said. But he could see Patrick was like a rubber ball — the harder you knocked him down, the faster and higher he bounced back.

The wonderful day came when the class was taken to the zoo. Even Harry Biggs, who usually made fun of school outings, looked forward to this one.

Off they went in the school bus, and Mr. Porter took them around.

"Like the Pied Piper of Hamelin," said Patrick, "with all the rats following him."

"Who are you calling a rat, Ginger?" asked Harry Biggs sourly.

Everywhere at the zoo was the smell of animals, birds, and straw. They had a map which showed them the quickest way to go around the zoo. The first lot of cages they went past held birds. There were all sizes and colors of birds from vultures to canaries. One cage

held several bright parrots. The parrots watched the children pass with round, wise eyes. Then, suddenly, the biggest and brightest of the lot flew from its perch and clung to the wire peering out at them.

"Patrick! Hello, Patrick dear!" it said. "Hello! Hello! Hello, Patrick! Hello, dear!"

Mr. Porter looked at Patrick.

"Oh, yes," he said. "I forgot about you, Patrick. It's a bit of a busman's holiday for you, isn't it?"

As they walked away, the parrot went on screaming after them, "Hello, Patrick! Patrick! Hello, dear!" in its funny, parrot voice.

On they went past the lions and tigers. Len and Graham stole sideways glances at Patrick, and so did Harry Biggs and several other children. Patrick looked as wide-eyed and interested as anyone else. He did not seem to see the glances at all.

They went past the bear pits, and then up a hill where there was nothing but trees. Among the trees, beside a stone fence, was a little house. On one of the gate posts was a brass peacock, polished

75

until it shone, and below that was a little notice saying *Head Keeper's Cottage*.

Now, for the first time, Patrick suddenly turned and grinned at Graham.

"*That's* where I live," he whispered.

They were looking into the bear pits ten minutes later when a man came hurrying to meet them. He was wearing lots of gold braid all over his blue uniform. There was gold braid around his cap, and his brass buttons shone like little suns. His eyes were blue and bright and his face was covered with freckles — more freckles than face, you might have said. He stopped to speak to Mr. Porter and took off his cap.

His hair was as red as fire.

"Is *that* your father?" Graham asked.

"Yes," said Patrick. "See, I told you he wore a lot of gold."

"Huh!" said Harry Biggs. "Well, why didn't you say when I asked you. . . . Why didn't you say he was a keeper at the zoo?"

"Head Keeper!" said Graham, feeling suddenly very proud of Patrick.

"Ordinary keepers don't have gold on their uniforms," Patrick pointed out.

"Why didn't you say?" Harry repeated. "Trying to be clever, eh?"

"I don't like things to sound too ordinary," said Patrick, sounding rather self-satisfied. "I like them to be noble and sort of mysterious."

"Well, you're mad," said Harry. But no one took any notice of him. Mr. Porter and Mr. O'Donnell — Head Keeper — joined them.

"This is Mr. O'Donnell," said Mr. Porter. "He has offered to let us have a look at the young lion cubs. They aren't on view to the public yet, so we are very lucky. And don't worry — the mother lion won't be there, so none of you will get eaten."

As they went on their way a little girl, who should have known better, said to Patrick, "Have you any other relatives who do interesting things, Patrick?"

"Are you mad?" cried Graham. But it was too late.

"My uncle," said Patrick without any hesitation. "Though he's really my great-uncle. He eats razor blades for a living, razor blades and burning matches."

"No one can eat razor blades!" shouted Harry Biggs.

"Well, my great-uncle does," said Patrick, and this time everyone believed him.

PS Patrick's great-uncle was a magician.

Looking for a Ghost

Running along the footpath, fire in his feet, came Sammy Scarlet. He ran on his toes, leaping as he ran, so that he seemed to dance and spin through the twilight like a gray, tumbling bird learning to fly. Sammy leaped as he ran, to keep himself brave. He was going to a haunted house. That evening he was going to see a ghost for the first time in his life.

The haunted house was on the edge of the city. It was the last house left in the street, and it was falling to pieces in the middle of a garden of weeds. The glass in the windows was broken, and some of the windows were boarded up. There was a tall fence around it, but in some places even the fence was tumbling down.

"They'll put a bulldozer through that old place soon," the man in the shop at the corner had said. "It's on valuable land, commercial land."

"Is it haunted?" Sammy had asked.

"They say there's a ghost, but it only comes out in the evening after the shops have closed and most people have gone home. I've never seen it," the man in the corner shop had replied, "and I'm not hanging around here after five-thirty just to watch some ghost. Only a little one too, they say."

"A twilight ghost," Sammy said to himself, and felt as if something breathed cold on the back of his neck, and whispered with cold lips in his ear.

Now, he ran swiftly through the early evening. Sammy had chosen his time carefully . . . not so dark that his mother would worry about him, not too light for a small, cold ghost.

Just a quick prowl around! thought Sammy, as he ran and leaped to keep away the fear which ran beside him like a chilly, pale-eyed dog.

If I go back now, I'm a coward, he thought, and leaped again. I've promised myself to see a ghost and I'm *going* to see a ghost.

He knew the street well, but evening changed it. It took him by surprise, seeming to have grown longer and emptier. And at the very end, the haunted house was waiting. Sammy could see its gate and its tired tumbledown fence. By the gate something moved softly. Sammy leaped in his running, matching his jump to the

jump of his heart. But the shadow by the gate was only a little girl bouncing a ball with a stick. She looked up as Sammy came running toward her.

"Hello," she said. "I thought no one ever came here in the evening."

"I've come," Sammy answered, panting. "I'm going to see the ghost."

The little girl looked at him with shadowy black eyes. "A real ghost?" she asked. "What ghost?"

"A ghost that haunts this house," Sammy replied. He was glad of someone to talk to, even a girl with a striped rubber ball in one hand and a stick in the other. She looked back at the house.

"Is this house haunted?" she asked again. "I suppose it looks a bit haunted. There are cobwebs inside, and thistles in the garden. Aren't you frightened of the ghost, then?"

"I'm not scared of ghosts," said Sammy cheerfully. (He hoped he sounded cheerful.) "They can be pretty scary to some people but, I don't know how it is, somehow they don't scare me. I'm going through the fence to take a look. They say it is only a little one."

"Why don't you try the gate?" suggested the girl, pushing at the gate with her stick. It creaked open. Sammy stared.

"That's funny," he said. "I looked at the gate earlier and it was locked."

"I'll come with you," said the girl. "My name is Belinda, and I would like to see a ghost too."

"I don't think you'd better," replied Sammy, frowning, "because ghosts can be pretty horrible, you know . . . with sharp teeth and claws and cackling laughs. Bony, too!"

"There's nothing wrong with being bony," said Belinda.

She was very thin with a pale, serious face and long brown hair. Though she did not smile she looked friendly and interested. Her heavy shoes made her legs look even thinner, and her dress was too

big for her, Sammy thought. Certainly it was too long, giving her an old-fashioned look.

"If it's scary to be bony," said Belinda, "I might frighten the ghost. Anyway, the gate is open and I can go in if I want to." She stepped into the old garden and Sammy followed her, half cross because she was coming into his private adventure, half pleased to have company. As he came through the gate Sammy felt a cold breath fall on the back of his neck. Turning around slowly he saw nothing. Perhaps it was just a little cool wind sliding into the empty garden with them.

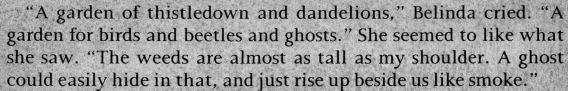

"A garden of thistledown and dandelions," Belinda cried. "A garden for birds and beetles and ghosts." She seemed to like what she saw. "The weeds are almost as tall as my shoulder. A ghost could easily hide in that, and just rise up beside us like smoke."

Sammy glanced thoughtfully at the grass, half expecting a smoky shape to billow up and wave its arms at him. But — no smoke, no sound. It was all very still. He could hear cars out on the main road, but they seemed like thin dreams of sound, tiny flies buzzing far away. He walked up the brick path and stood on the front steps of the haunted house, looking at its sad veranda. One of the carved posts was crumbling down and the veranda sagged with it.

"You'd feel cruel just standing on this veranda," Sammy remarked. "It looks so limp and sick."

"Cruelty to verandas!" said Belinda seriously. "Stand on it lightly, Sammy, and we'll go inside. I think a ghost would be more likely to be inside, don't you?"

"The door will be locked, won't it?" Sammy suggested. Then, "How did you know my name?" he asked, looking puzzled.

"You *look* like a Sammy," was all she said. She pushed the door and it slowly opened, like a black mouth opening to suck them into its shadows.

"I might stay out here," Sammy said. "The floor could cave in or something." His voice was quiet and squashed small by the heavy silence of the whole house and garden.

"You don't have to be afraid," Belinda told him kindly. "It's just an old, empty house, and old houses were made of good wood." Through the dark door she slid and vanished. Sammy *had* to follow her. Then he had the most terrible fright. He was standing in a hall so dim and dusty that he could see almost nothing. But what he could see was a dim and dusty figure at the other end of the hall moving slowly toward him.

"The ghost!" cried Sammy.

Belinda looked back at him. He could not see her face properly, but for some reason he thought she might be smiling.

"It isn't a ghost," she told him. "It's a mirror. There's a tall cupboard at the end with a mirror in its door. It's your own reflection that's frightening you."

Sammy blinked and saw that what she said could be true. They walked cautiously up the hall. The mirror reflected the open doorway behind them. It was so dark inside that the evening outside looked bright and pearly.

Sammy rubbed his finger across the mirror.

The mirror moved and they heard a low moaning.

"The ghost!" gasped Sammy again, but it was just the cupboard door. It was open a little bit, and creaked when Sammy touched it.

"Come upstairs!" Belinda said. "They were nice, once, these stairs. They used to be polished every day."

"How do you know?" asked Sammy, looking up the dark stairway.

"They are smooth under the dust," Belinda replied, "smooth with feet walking, and hands polishing. But that was a long time ago."

"How can you see your way upstairs?" Sammy asked. "It's so dark."

"There's enough light," she answered, already several steps above him. Sammy followed her. Out of the dark came a hand, soft and silent as the shadows, a hand that laid silken fingers across his face.

"The ghost!" cried Sammy for the third time.

"Cobwebs, only cobwebs!" called Belinda. Sammy touched his face. His own fingers, stiff with fright, found only cobwebs, just as Belinda had said. He stumbled and scrambled up after her on to the landing. The only window was boarded over. But it was easy to peep through the cracks and look over the thistly garden and down the empty street.

"There used to be grass there," Belinda whispered, peering out. "Grass and cows. But that was a long time ago." She straightened up. "Come through *this* door," she said in her ordinary voice.

Sammy did not want to be left behind. They went through the door into a small room. Here, the boards had partly slipped away

from the windows. Evening light brightened the walls and striped the ceiling. There were the remains of green curtains and a rocking chair with one rocker broken. Sitting in the chair was a very old doll. It looked as if someone had put it down and had gone out to play for a moment. The doll seemed to expect someone to play with it. Sammy looked over to the doll and around the room, and then out through the window. "There's no ghost," he said, "and it's getting late. I'll have to be going."

The ghost did not seem as important as it had a moment ago, but Sammy thought he would remember the silent, tumbling house and its wild garden long after he had stopped thinking about ghosts.

They went down the stairs again and Sammy did not jump at the cobwebs. They went past the mirror, and he creaked the cupboard door on purpose this time. Now, the sound did not frighten him. It was gentle and complaining, not fierce or angry.

"It only wants to be left alone," Belinda said, and that was what it had sounded like.

They walked down the hall and Sammy turned to wave good-bye

to his reflection before he shut the door. The reflection waved back at him from the end of a long tunnel of shadow. Outside, the evening darkened. Stars were showing.

"No ghost!" said Sammy, shaking his head.

They walked to the gate.

"Will you be coming back some other night to look for the ghost?" Belinda asked.

"I don't think so," Sammy answered. "I don't really believe in ghosts. I just thought there might be one. I've looked once, and there isn't one, and that's enough."

He turned to run home, but something made him stop and look sharply at Belinda.

"Did you see *your* reflection in that mirror?" he asked curiously. "I don't remember seeing your reflection."

Belinda did not answer his question. Instead she asked him one of her own.

"Everyone has a reflection, don't they?" It was hard to see her in the late evening, but once again Sammy thought she might be smiling.

"You went up the stairs first," he went on. "Why didn't you brush the cobwebs away?"

"I'm not as tall as you," Belinda said.

Sammy peered at her, waiting for her to say something more. Just for a moment, very faintly, he felt that chilly breeze touch the back of his neck again.

"No ghost!" he said at last. "No such thing as ghosts!" Then, without saying good-bye, he ran off, rockets in the heels of his shoes.

Belinda watched him go.

"The question is," she said to herself, "whether he would recognize a ghost, supposing he saw one."

She went back through the gate and locked it carefully after her. She was already faint and far off in the evening, and as she pushed the bolt in place she disappeared entirely.